MR. CHARLES'
CORNBREAD

MARLON WADE

MR. CHARLES' CORNBREAD

THE FIRST VISIT

CHAPTER 1

The summer after third grade had just begun, and Eddie was sure it was going to be the most boring one yet. He sat cross-legged on the floor of his room, tossing a rubber ball against the wall, the hollow thunk echoing in the quiet house. All his friends had scattered to far-off camps or were visiting family out of state, leaving him behind with nothing but time.

"Eddie! Come grab your bag!" Mama's voice floated up the stairs, breaking his train of thought. Eddie let out a loud sigh, tossed his ball onto the bed, and grabbed his backpack from the corner. As he stuffed his sketchpad inside, he glanced at the poster of a rocket ship on his wall, wishing he could launch himself anywhere but wherever Mama was dragging him. His sneakers dragged against the carpet as he trudged downstairs, the aroma of frying onions meeting him halfway.

Downstairs, Eddie paused in the doorway, watching Mama as she moved about the kitchen with practiced ease. He could tell she was in a hurry, but there was something else too—an energy in her movements that made him think she cared about these visits more than she let on. He slumped against the counter.

"Mama, why are we visiting him?" Eddie asked, curiosity tinged with mild frustration.

Mama wiped her hands on a towel, her movements slowing just a bit before she placed a bag of rice on the counter. "Because it's the right thing to do. Mr. Charles doesn't have many people checking on him, and it's important to look after folks when they get older."

Eddie crossed his arms. "But why me?"

Mama smiled, soft but firm. "Because one day, you'll understand what it means to be there for someone who needs it. And because it's good for you too, baby. It's good to learn from people who have lived a lot of life."

Eddie sighed, shifting his weight and tapping his fingers against the counter. Maybe if he stalled long enough, Mama would forget about taking him. But one glance at her determined face told him there was no way out. He knew arguing wouldn't get him anywhere. "Fine," he mumbled, grabbing his backpack. Mama gave him a knowing look before handing him a small paper bag to carry.

"Where are we going?" Eddie asked as he followed her to the car, still dragging his feet.

"To Mr. Charles' house," Mama replied, her voice firm but with a familiar warmth that meant there was no room for debate. Eddie knew better than to argue when Mama used that tone. She wasn't harsh, but when she made up her mind, it was final. It was the kind of authority that came from years of keeping their small family running smoothly, and Eddie didn't dare test it now. "And hurry up!"

Eddie hesitated at the doorway, confused. "Who's Mr. Charles?" he mumbled under his breath. Still, he grabbed his backpack, shoving a book and his sketchpad inside. Staying home wasn't an option.

As they drove through their neighborhood, Eddie stared out the window, watching as the familiar streets gave way to rows of older houses. Paint peeled off their shutters, and weeds pushed through cracked driveways. Mama kept her hands steady on the steering wheel, humming softly to herself.

"Mama, why are we going to his house?" Eddie finally asked, leaning forward to peer at her.

"Because Mr. Charles needs a little help," Mama said simply. "He's a good man, but he's been on his own for a long time. I check in on him, and now you'll come with me."

Eddie frowned, kicking his feet against the glove compartment. "Doesn't he have a family?"

Mama's humming stopped, and her expression turned thoughtful. She rubbed her thumb over the steering wheel before speaking, as if recalling something from long ago. Her hands tightened briefly on the steering wheel, and her gaze softened as she looked straight ahead. It was as though she was sifting through her thoughts, trying to find the right words, but all she said was, "He has family. But sometimes people get busy, and folks like Mr. Charles don't get visited as much as they should."

The car turned into a gravel driveway, and Eddie's eyes widened. His heart thudded as he took in the house looming ahead of them. It looked like it belonged in a ghost story, and he couldn't stop his thoughts from spiraling. What kind of man lived here? Would he be as scary as the house itself? The house was bigger than he expected, but its faded paint and sagging porch gave it an almost haunted look. The yard was overgrown with weeds, some reaching nearly to Eddie's knees, and an old tire swing hung crookedly from a tree, swaying slightly in the breeze as though moved by an invisible hand. Vines crept up the sides of the house, curling around the wooden beams like fingers, gripping the structure as if refusing to let go. The porch steps sagged under their weight, and a shutter hung loose, clinging stubbornly to its rusted hinges.

Mama pulled into the driveway and put the car in park, but she didn't get out right away. She exhaled, glancing at the house as if seeing it for the first time in years. Then, she grabbed a paper bag from the backseat, the weight making her arm dip slightly as the cans inside clinked together. "Come on," she said, her voice encouraging. "Don't keep me waiting."

Eddie slid out of the car, the gravel crunching under his sneakers. He followed behind her slowly, glancing around the overgrown yard. "Mama," he whispered, tugging at her sleeve, "this place looks spooky."

Mama chuckled. "It's just old, baby. Nothing to be scared of."

She knocked on the door, the sharp sound breaking the eerie quiet. Eddie jumped, his nerves tightening like a coiled spring. The house seemed to inhale, settling into itself as though it knew company had arrived. They stood in silence for a moment, the creak of the old house blending with the faint rustle of leaves outside. Eddie shifted nervously, his eyes darting to a cracked window near the door. Inside, shadows moved, and then a soft shuffle of feet approached. When the door creaked open, he froze. Standing there was a man taller than anyone Eddie had ever seen, his frame broad but slightly hunched. His face was lined, and his gray eyes seemed to pierce through the dim light of the house.

Mr. Charles looked at Mama, his expression shifting just slightly, as if he was deciding whether to let them in. His fingers flexed at his sides before he cleared his throat. Then, his sharp but tired gray eyes settled on Eddie, studying him in silence. He lingered there, as if searching for something in the boy's face. After what felt like forever, he gave a slow, deliberate nod and stepped aside, disappearing into the dimly lit house without a word.

"Come on," Mama said, nudging Eddie gently forward. Eddie hesitated, gripping the straps of his bag as he stepped into the house.

The inside was dim, the curtains drawn over the windows, casting long, shadowy shapes across the floor. Eddie felt a chill run down his spine as his eyes adjusted to the gloom. The faint creak of the wooden boards beneath his sneakers echoed in the silence, and the shadows seemed to shift slightly as if alive. The smell of something warm and buttery teased his senses, mixing with the sharper scent of dust, making him feel both curious and uneasy.

"Go sit at the table," Mama said, motioning toward the kitchen. Eddie shuffled toward a wooden chair, sitting on the very edge of it. He watched as Mr. Charles moved toward the stove, his large hands adjusting the flame under a cast-iron skillet.

"Charles, I brought the groceries you asked for," Mama said as she set the bag on the counter. "And Eddie's going to be coming with me this summer."

Eddie's stomach tightened. Spend the summer here? The quiet house felt too heavy, and Mr. Charles barely seemed to notice him. He glanced at Mama, who was now unpacking cans and bread.

Mr. Charles finally spoke, his voice low and rough like gravel. "Hmph."

Eddie swallowed, suddenly aware of how small his voice felt in the heavy silence of the house. He wanted to ask Mama why they had to stay, but something about Mr. Charles' gaze kept him from speaking. Eddie wasn't so sure. He stared at the scratched surface of the table, his thoughts swirling with unease and curiosity. What kind of summer was this going to be?

A SEAT AT THE TABLE

The gravel crunched beneath their tires as Mama backed out of the driveway, and Eddie stole one last glance at the house. Its crooked shutters and overgrown porch seemed to lean toward him, like it had secrets it wasn't ready to share. The vines curling up the porch posts swayed gently in the breeze, as though waving him goodbye—or maybe daring him to return. Eddie felt a strange mix of relief and unease as they drove away. The house's quiet weight still pressed on him, and he couldn't shake the thought that it held stories it wasn't ready to tell. Yet, as the house faded from view, Eddie found himself wishing he had just a few more seconds to look at it.

In the car, the silence stretched long, broken only by the hum of the engine and the faint chirping of birds outside. Eddie shifted in his seat, fiddling with the strap of his book bag. The lingering smell of Mr. Charles' house clung to his clothes—warm and buttery but also dusty, like old papers left in an attic too long. It made his nose itch.

"Well?" Mama finally broke the silence, her tone light but probing. "What did you think of Mr. Charles?"

Eddie hesitated, his fingers still tugging at the fraying edge of his bag strap. "He's... big," he said, though that didn't feel like the right word. "And quiet."

Mama chuckled softly, glancing at him out of the corner of her eye. "He's not so bad, baby. Just takes some time to warm up to."

"But why doesn't his family visit him?" Eddie asked, his voice quieter this time, almost as though he were afraid of the answer.

Eddie glanced at her, wanting to ask more but something in the way her fingers gripped the wheel told him not to. Mama's hands tightened slightly on the steering wheel, her knuckles whitening for a brief moment. Her lips pressed together, as though she was weighing her words carefully. "You know," she said finally, her voice quieter now, "sometimes it's not just about being busy. Some folks find it hard to face what's been left behind."

Eddie turned his gaze to the window, watching the trees blur past. "Does he like us coming over? But what he really wanted to ask was—had Mr. Charles always been like this? Why did he even care? It wasn't like he wanted to be there. But the way Mr. Charles had looked at him—like he saw something Eddie couldn't—made it hard to ignore. Or was he waiting for something… or someone?" he asked after a pause.

Mama smiled faintly, her expression a mix of patience and something deeper—something Eddie couldn't quite name. "He wouldn't say it, but I think he does."

When they pulled into their driveway, the familiar scent of dinner greeted them. Eddie's stomach rumbled as he climbed out of the car, the warm smell of spices and cooking meat wrapping around him like a hug. From inside, the faint bubbling of the stew and the soft clatter of a wooden spoon against the pot drifted out to meet him. Steam curled lazily upward from the kitchen window, hinting at the comforting meal waiting inside. Inside, his dad stood at the counter, stirring a pot of something that looked thick and hearty.

"How'd it go?" Dad asked, his eyes flicking between Mama and Eddie as they walked in.

Eddie hesitated, kicking off his shoes by the door. "Okay, I guess," he said finally, his voice trailing off.

Mama smiled knowingly, setting the grocery bag on the counter. "He's nervous," she explained to Dad. "Mr. Charles can be a lot at first."

Dad nodded, his expression understanding. "You'll get used to it, bud," he said, ladling some stew into a bowl. "Just takes time."

As they sat down to eat, Eddie pushed the food around his plate, his thoughts drifting back to the heavy silence of Mr. Charles' house. It wasn't just the house that felt quiet—it was Mr. Charles himself. His gruff demeanor and sparse words left so much unsaid, and Eddie found himself wondering what stories might be hiding behind those deep-set eyes and lined face.

"What's on your mind?" Dad asked, pulling Eddie from his thoughts. "You've barely touched your food."

Eddie shrugged. "I was just thinking about Mr. Charles." His quietness wasn't like anything Eddie had encountered before. It wasn't just silence—it was as if Mr. Charles held back an entire world of stories and memories behind those deep, guarded eyes. Eddie couldn't help but wonder what had made him that way and why he seemed so different from anyone else he'd ever met.

Mama and Dad exchanged a glance—one that seemed to hold more than words. 'You'll figure him out,' Mama said gently, though there was something almost wistful in her voice. 'Just give it time.'

Later that evening, Eddie sat on the edge of his bed, his sketchpad balanced on his knees. He tried to draw Mr. Charles' house, but every time he started, the lines came out wrong—too crooked, too dark. With a huff, Eddie scratched out the lopsided house and flipped the page. His pencil hovered, hesitating—then he started on the cast-iron skillet instead. At least that made sense. its edges smooth and sturdy, the way it had looked sitting on Mr. Charles' stove.

He stared at the drawing, his pencil hovering above the paper. The smell of the house seemed to linger in his nose—a rich, savory aroma, layered with a hint of sweetness, yet shadowed by something older and harder to define, like history clinging to its walls. Eddie set the pencil down and sighed, leaning back against the wall.

He wasn't sure if he wanted to go back. But at the same time, a small part of him—one he couldn't quite ignore—was curious to see what he might uncover. Was it the mystery of Mr. Charles, with his quiet, gruff presence? Or the strange pull of the house itself, with its heavy air and faint aroma of toasted cornmeal and something almost earthy, like the past lingering in the present? "Whatever it was, it tugged at him, making it impossible to let go. Eddie shut the sketchbook with a firm snap. He didn't have to go back. It wasn't his problem. But even as he thought it, he knew he wasn't fooling himself.

THE SECOND TRIP

Eddie sat in the back seat of Mama's car, his legs swinging slightly as he stared out the window. It was their second trip to Mr. Charles' house, and the nervous feeling in his stomach hadn't gone away. He drummed his fingers against his knee, shifting in his seat. Maybe today would be different. Maybe it wouldn't. Either way, he couldn't shake the feeling that something about this visit mattered in a way he didn't understand yet. The house had left a mark on him—its quiet weight, the way it seemed to watch him through its sagging shutters. He couldn't explain it, but it felt like stepping back inside would uncover something he wasn't ready to face, even if part of him wanted to. Instead, it felt heavier, like the house had somehow reached out and grabbed hold of him during their last visit.

The warm morning light filtered through the trees, casting dappled shadows on the road ahead. Mama hummed softly to herself, her hands steady on the steering wheel. "You feeling alright, baby?" she asked, glancing at him in the rearview mirror.

Eddie shrugged. "I guess."

Mama didn't press further, but the corners of her mouth lifted in a knowing smile. "You'll see. It gets easier."

As they turned into the gravel driveway, Eddie caught sight of the house again. It hadn't changed—the same sagging porch, the same creeping vines—but it didn't feel quite as menacing this time. The crooked tire swing in the front yard swayed gently in the breeze, and Eddie wondered if it had ever carried the weight of laughter or if it had always hung there in silence.

The air smelled different here, carrying the earthy aroma of damp wood mingled with a faint sweetness, like toasted grains. It was a scent that hinted at something both rustic and familiar, settling in the air heavier and richer than it did at home. Eddie stepped out of the car, his sneakers crunching against the gravel, and followed Mama up the porch steps. The screen door creaked as she knocked, its sound sharp and drawn out, like an old voice straining to be heard. For a moment, all Eddie could hear was the distant chirping of birds and the faint rustle of leaves, their softness a stark contrast to the house's imposing stillness, as though nature itself hesitated to intrude.

When the door opened, Mr. Charles was there, just as tall and imposing as Eddie remembered. But this time, Eddie noticed something different. The lines on Mr. Charles' face didn't seem as sharp, and his shoulders didn't slump quite as much. His gray eyes flicked to Eddie briefly before turning to Mama. Stepping inside, Eddie felt the shift immediately. The air was cooler, heavier, carrying the scent of flour and something faintly smoky. The outside world—chirping birds, rustling leaves—seemed to disappear as the door creaked shut behind them.

Eddie followed Mama into the house, his steps cautious but less hesitant than before. The air inside carried the same mix of scents—something warm and inviting, like freshly baked bread, mingled with the dusty stillness of forgotten corners. Eddie wrinkled his nose but didn't say anything.

"Good morning, Charles," Mama said, her tone bright as she set the grocery bag on the counter. "How you feeling today?"

Mr. Charles grunted in response, a sound that Eddie was beginning to understand wasn't as unfriendly as it seemed. He watched as Mr. Charles moved to the stove; his large hands steady as he adjusted the flame under a cast-iron skillet. The soft sizzle of something cooking reached Eddie's ears, and his curiosity piqued.

"What's that?" Eddie blurted out before he could stop himself.

Mr. Charles glanced at him, his expression unreadable. "Cornbread," he said simply, his voice low and gravelly.

Eddie blinked. Cornbread? That was the smell he couldn't get out of his head last time. "Is it... for breakfast?"

Mr. Charles didn't answer right away. He gave the skillet a careful shake, the golden edges of the batter beginning to curl away from the sides. "It's for whenever," he said finally.

Mama chuckled as she unpacked the groceries. "Mr. Charles makes the best cornbread, don't you, Charles?"

Another grunt, this one softer. Eddie leaned forward slightly, watching the skillet with growing interest. He didn't know much about cooking, but there was something fascinating about the way Mr. Charles worked—how his hands moved with precision, how the smell of the cornbread filled the room without trying too hard.

As Mama finished putting things away, she turned to Eddie. "Why don't you take a seat at the table?" she suggested. "Give Mr. Charles some room."

Eddie nodded, sliding into the same chair he'd sat in last time. The wood felt cool against his palms as he gripped the edges, his gaze wandering around the kitchen. He felt a little less like an outsider this time, but the room's heavy silence still pressed on him, making him wonder what stories these walls might hold—and whether he was ready to hear them. From here, he could see more of the kitchen—the worn edges of the counters, the faint scratches on the wooden floor, the faded wallpaper curling slightly at the edges. It was a kitchen that felt lived in, like it had been a witness to years of meals and conversations, though Eddie had a feeling it had been quiet for a long time.

Mr. Charles flipped the cornbread onto a plate, the golden crust glistening slightly. He cut a small piece and set it on a napkin, sliding it across the counter toward Eddie. "Taste," he said.

Eddie froze. He hadn't expected this. He glanced at Mama, who gave him an encouraging nod. Slowly, he reached for the napkin, the warmth of the cornbread seeping through the paper.

The first bite was a surprise. The outside was crisp, but the inside was soft and light, with a subtle sweetness that lingered on his tongue. Eddie's eyes widened. "This is really good," he said, his voice full of wonder.

Mr. Charles didn't say anything, but a faint smile tugged at the corner of his mouth. Mama laughed softly. "Told you," she said, handing Mr. Charles a cup of coffee. "You've got a fan now."

Eddie took another bite, savoring the flavors. He wanted to ask how it was made, but something told him not to. For now, it was enough to sit in the quiet kitchen, the smell of fresh cornbread in the air, and the faintest hint of warmth in Mr. Charles' otherwise stoic demeanor. But as he finished the last bite, a question lingered—how long had it been since Mr. Charles had shared his cornbread with someone else? And why did that thought make Eddie's chest feel tight?

SILENT STORIES

Eddie couldn't stop thinking about Mr. Charles' house. It stayed with him in the quiet moments, like an itch he couldn't quite scratch. It wasn't just a house—it was a feeling. A weight that had settled in his chest, making him want to look away but keeping him coming back. The way the shadows seemed to shift in its dim corners and the faint, lingering aroma of something baked and forgotten haunted his thoughts. It wasn't just the house itself—it was the feeling it left behind, as though it held secrets waiting for him to uncover. At school, he found himself doodling its crooked shutters in the margins of his notebook, and at night, he replayed the faint creak of the screen door in his mind. Something about it drew him in, even though he didn't fully understand why.

At home, Mama was bustling about the kitchen, humming a soft tune while Eddie leaned against the counter, watching her stir a pot of soup. The scent of simmering broth and warm spices wrapped around him, comforting and familiar. "Mama," he started, hesitating, "why doesn't Mr. Charles ever talk much?"

Mama paused, her wooden spoon hovering over the pot as she looked at him. Her brows knitted together slightly, and her lips pressed into a thoughtful line, as if searching for the right words. For a moment, the warmth of the kitchen seemed to hold her in quiet reflection. "He talks when he has something to say," she replied gently. "Some folks don't fill the air with words unless they think it's worth it."

"But doesn't it feel... lonely?" Eddie asked, frowning.

Mama gave him a small smile, reaching out to tousle his hair. "Maybe," she admitted. "But Mr. Charles has lived a lot of life, baby. Sometimes that leaves a person with more to think about than to say."

Eddie didn't respond, but the weight of her words settled in his chest. He couldn't imagine not talking about the things that mattered most. Did Mr. Charles keep it all bottled up? Or was he just waiting for the right person to listen?

The next day, Eddie met his friend Jamal at the park. They climbed onto the swings, their feet kicking at the dusty ground below. "You're awful quiet today," Jamal said, glancing at Eddie as he pumped his legs to swing higher.

"Just thinking," Eddie mumbled.

"About what?" Jamal asked, leaning back and gripping the chains of his swing.

Eddie hesitated. "About this guy my mama works for," he said finally. "Mr. Charles."

Jamal's eyebrows lifted. 'That old guy? Isn't he, like, super scary?' His voice hushed, like he was telling one of those ghost stories kids whispered at sleepovers. 'I heard he doesn't like people bothering him. Like, ever.' His voice dropped slightly, as if he were sharing a spooky secret, and he glanced over his shoulder, as though Mr. Charles might suddenly appear behind them.

Eddie frowned, kicking at the dirt. 'He's not scary,' he said defensively. 'He's just... different. You ever think some people just don't want to be around a lot of noise?' "Just... different."

Jamal smirked. "Different how?"

"He doesn't talk much," Eddie admitted. "And his house is kinda old and weird. But he makes cornbread, and it smells amazing."

"Cornbread?" Jamal laughed. "That's random."

"It's not random," Eddie said, a little too sharply. "It's... good."

Jamal shrugged. "Sounds boring to me.

Eddie didn't answer. But later that night, as he sat on the back porch with his sketchpad, he realized he wasn't done thinking about it."

It bugged him, more than it should've. Mr. Charles wasn't just some boring old man—he was something else. But how could Eddie explain that when he didn't fully understand it himself? Mr. Charles wasn't boring—he was something else entirely. It was the way he carried himself, like he knew things Eddie couldn't even imagine, and the quiet stillness that seemed to hold more stories than words ever could. Eddie couldn't quite put it into words, but he felt there was a depth to Mr. Charles that made him want to keep looking closer.

That evening, after dinner, Eddie wandered outside and sat on the back porch, his sketchpad resting on his knees. The crickets hummed in the thick summer air, and a faint breeze carried the scent of cut grass. He stared at the page, the tip of his pencil hovering. This time, he tried to draw Mr. Charles. He started with the broad shoulders, the deep-set eyes, and the lines that etched his face like a map of all the things he'd seen. But no matter how hard he tried, the picture felt incomplete, like he was missing something important.

With a huff, Eddie scratched out the lopsided lines and flipped the page. His pencil hovered, hesitating—then he started again, slower this time, like he was trying to see beneath the surface of Mr. Charles' face. No matter how hard he tried, he couldn't get it right. Maybe it wasn't just his drawing—maybe it was Mr. Charles himself. Some things just stayed hidden, no matter how hard you looked. What was it about Mr. Charles that made him so hard to figure out? Eddie didn't have the answer, but he knew one thing: he wanted to keep trying to understand. And maybe, just maybe, Mr. Charles wanted to be understood, too.

LESSONS

MR. CHARLES' CORNBREAD

Eddie's visits to Mr. Charles' house were starting to feel less like chores and more like stepping into a new world. Each time they went, Eddie noticed something different—the way the light hit the old photographs on the mantle, the quiet rhythm of Mr. Charles' movements, or the ever-present aroma of food that seemed to define the house. He had never paid attention to details like this before, but something about Mr. Charles' home made him look closer, listen harder. Yet, now and then, Eddie noticed how Mr. Charles paused a little longer, his movements just a touch slower than before.

One morning, as Mama packed the car with groceries for their trip, Eddie slipped into the passenger seat without complaint. He stared out the window, watching the familiar streets roll by, but his thoughts drifted elsewhere. He wondered if Mr. Charles had always lived in that house, if he had once shared it with someone. The house didn't feel abandoned, but it didn't feel full either. It was like it was waiting, holding onto something Eddie couldn't quite name. "You're getting used to this, huh?" Mama asked with a knowing smile.

Eddie shrugged, but the corner of his mouth lifted slightly. "I guess."

When they arrived, the house looked the same as always, but Eddie found himself stepping onto the porch with less hesitation. The familiar creak of the screen door welcomed them as Mr. Charles opened it. He nodded at Mama and glanced at Eddie before shuffling back inside. The shuffle was barely noticeable before, but now Eddie saw the deliberate effort behind each step. For the first time, Eddie noticed the way Mr. Charles' hand gripped the edge of the counter—just for a second—before he straightened himself.

Eddie followed, feeling a little more at ease as he sat at the table. Mr. Charles was already at the stove, his back turned, the cast-iron skillet resting on the burner. Eddie thought he heard a faint sigh as Mr. Charles adjusted the flame, a sound so small he wondered if he imagined it.

"What's he making this time?" Eddie asked, his curiosity bubbling to the surface.

Mama chuckled as she began unpacking the groceries. "You know what it is."

"Cornbread?" Eddie guessed, leaning forward slightly.

Mr. Charles grunted, which Eddie had come to understand as his version of a "yes."

The golden aroma filled the kitchen, and Eddie watched as Mr. Charles moved with quiet precision, flipping the cornbread onto a plate. It was a ritual, Eddie realized—something steady and unchanging in a house that seemed full of memories.

"Here," Mr. Charles said gruffly, sliding a piece across the table toward Eddie.

Eddie hesitated for only a moment before picking it up. He thought about asking how Mr. Charles had learned to make cornbread like this—who had taught him, if it had always been a part of his life—but the question stuck in his throat. Instead, he focused on the warmth in his hands, the simple act of sharing a meal. When he took a bite, the flavors seemed to explode on his tongue—savory, sweet, and a subtle hint of something smoky and earthy, like it carried a whisper of stories from long ago.

"This is the best thing I've ever tasted," Eddie said, his voice full of wonder.

Mama smiled as she poured coffee for Mr. Charles. The kitchen had grown quiet, but it wasn't an uncomfortable silence. It was the kind that settled between people who didn't need to fill every space with words. "See? Told you."

Mr. Charles didn't say anything, but Eddie thought he saw the faintest flicker of pride in the older man's eyes. It was the smallest thing, just a shift in his expression, but it stayed with Eddie long after the last bite of cornbread was gone. That small glimmer made Eddie feel a connection, as if he'd been let in on a secret part of Mr. Charles. It wasn't just about the cornbread—it felt like being trusted, like Mr. Charles saw something in him worth sharing. Eddie didn't know why that mattered so much, but it did. Maybe Mr. Charles had spent too many years keeping things to himself. Maybe sharing something—even something as simple as cornbread—was harder than it looked.

Later that afternoon, as they loaded the empty grocery bags back into the car, Eddie glanced back at the house. He wondered what Mr. Charles did after they left, if the house fell back into silence the moment the door closed. Did he sit by the window? Read a book? Or just listen to the quiet? The air outside was thick with summer warmth, but inside that house, Eddie imagined the air was still, holding onto things left unsaid. Mr. Charles stood by the window; his silhouette framed by the curtains. For a moment, Eddie thought he saw Mr. Charles' hand lift slightly, but then it lowered again, as if the effort was just a little too much. Eddie didn't say anything to Mama, but he kept that image in his mind the whole ride home. Next time, maybe he'd say something. Maybe Mr. Charles would, too.

THE WEIGHT OF TIME

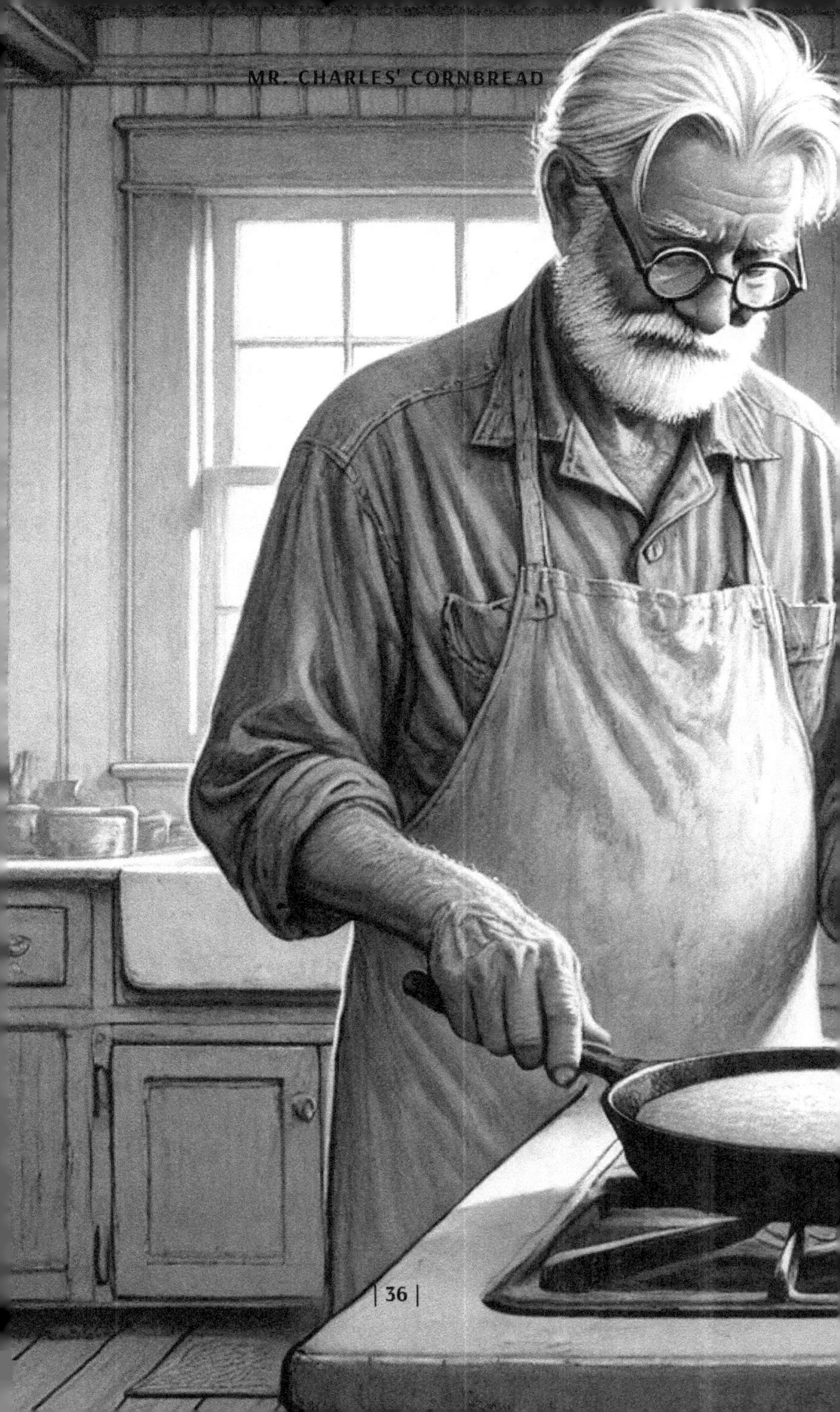

Eddie had just finished his second helping of corn-bread, his curiosity bubbling up again as he pushed the plate aside. The aroma still lingered in the air, mingling with the faint scent of coffee and the old wood of the kitchen.

"Mr. Charles," Eddie began, his voice hesitant but steady, "how did you learn to make cornbread like this?"

Mr. Charles, seated at the end of the table, raised an eyebrow and leaned back slightly. He took a long sip from his coffee cup, as if weighing whether to answer. Eddie waited, his hands folded tightly in his lap, the silence stretching just long enough for his cheeks to flush.

Finally, Mr. Charles set his mug down and glanced at Eddie. "My grandmother taught me," he said gruffly, the corners of his mouth pulling into the faintest hint of a smile. "She was one of those women who didn't need measuring cups. Said you had to know it by feel."

"By feel?" Eddie echoed, tilting his head.

"That's right," Mr. Charles said. He rested his broad hands on the table, fingers lightly tapping the wood. "She had me in the kitchen when I was no older than you. Kept me close, showing me how to sift the corn-meal just so, how to mix it smooth but not too thin. 'Pay attention,' she'd say. 'The cornbread will tell you when it's ready.'"

Eddie frowned. "What do you mean?"

Mr. Charles chuckled, low and rumbling, like he had just told himself a private joke. "Cornbread isn't some-thing you rush. You watch how it bubbles, listen for the sizzle, smell the crust when it's just turning golden. When you learn that, you don't need a recipe. You just know."

Eddie stared at him, his mind turning over the idea that cornbread could speak in its own way. "But how did you get so good at it?"

Mr. Charles' smile faded into a more reflective look. "Lots of practice," he said. "Plenty of mistakes, too. But it wasn't just about making it taste good. My grandmother used to tell me that cornbread was more than a side dish. It was comfort, something you shared with people to let them know they mattered. I guess I never forgot that."

For a moment, neither of them spoke. The only sound was the quiet hum of the kitchen, the faint clink of Mr. Charles setting his cup down. Eddie glanced at the empty plate in front of him, suddenly realizing that cornbread wasn't just food—it was a memory, a story, a way of keeping something alive.

Eddie traced his fingers along the rim of his plate, his mind still lingering on the words Mr. Charles had just spoken. He thought about the times Mama made cornbread at home; the way she always said her mother used to make it the same way. It made him wonder about all the hands that had mixed cornmeal and milk before them, each batch holding a little bit of the past, passed down without words. Maybe food wasn't just food—maybe it carried stories in the same way old houses and forgotten photographs did.

His gaze drifted toward the small window above the sink, where the late afternoon light spilled across the counter. He wondered if Mr. Charles had ever shared his cornbread with anyone else in this house—if, long before Eddie had ever stepped foot here, there had been another boy sitting at this same table, listening to the same quiet wisdom. That thought settled deep in his chest, warm and heavy, like the last bite of cornbread still lingering on his tongue.

Eddie nodded slowly, feeling like he'd just been let in on something special. He wanted to say something—to thank him, maybe—but the words didn't come. Instead, he just sat there, letting the warmth of the moment settle around him. Mr. Charles wasn't just making cornbread—he was passing along a piece of himself, just like his grandmother had done for him. And somehow, Eddie felt like he was part of that now, too. He thought about all the times he'd eaten cornbread before, never giving it much thought. But now, it felt different. It carried something more than just flavor—it carried a story, a history, and a quiet kind of love that didn't need to be spoken aloud.

MAMA'S MEMORIES

MARLON WA

Eddie had grown used to the rhythm of their visits; the way each week brought a new detail about Mr. Charles to light. But over time, he started noticing things he hadn't before. Mr. Charles still cooked, still greeted them at the door, but there was a difference in how he moved. He sat down more often now, resting after even small tasks. His voice, already low and gruff, seemed quieter, as if he spoke only when necessary. Eddie couldn't put a finger on it, but the man who had once seemed so solid and steady now seemed, somehow, more fragile.

Mama didn't say much about it, but Eddie caught the way she looked at Mr. Charles, the way she gently steered him to a chair if he stood too long. And Eddie, though he didn't fully understand, began to feel the weight of it. The house, too, seemed different. It was still the same house—dim, quiet, filled with the familiar smell of cornbread—but Eddie started noticing the dust gathering on shelves, the way a few more books leaned precariously against each other. It was as though the house itself was taking on Mr. Charles' weariness.

One afternoon, as Eddie sat at the table watching Mr. Charles at the stove, he found himself asking, "Mr. Charles, do you ever get tired of making cornbread?"

Mr. Charles glanced at him, a small smile playing on his lips. "Boy, you don't ever get tired of eating it, do you?"

Eddie grinned, but the question lingered. He watched as Mr. Charles turned back to the skillet, his movements deliberate, careful. When Mr. Charles finally handed him a piece, Eddie took a bite and realized it wasn't just the taste that made it special. It was the act itself—Mr. Charles making the cornbread, sharing it. It was a piece of him, something he could still give. And Eddie wondered—what happens when he can't? Will the kitchen feel the same without the sound of the skillet, without the scent of warm bread filling the air?

As the days stretched on, Eddie began to see Mr. Charles in a new light. He wasn't just the quiet man who made amazing cornbread. He was someone who carried a lifetime of stories, someone who had been strong and proud, and now, though he moved a little slower, he still found ways to give, to teach. And Eddie, sitting at that table week after week, started to realize he was learning more than he thought.

Mama, too, seemed to sense the changes.

One evening, on the drive home, Eddie finally asked, "Mama, how long have you known Mr. Charles?"

Mama was quiet for a moment, her hands steady on the wheel. "Since I was younger than you," she finally said. "My daddy used to bring me by to help out when Mr. Charles' wife was sick. He took care of her for a long time." She let out a quiet sigh, her fingers resting on the steering wheel as if the weight of memory was pressing down. "Back then, I didn't realize just how much he did for folks. It wasn't just about helping—it was about learning how to care for people, even in the smallest ways.

"One winter, when we didn't have much, he left a bag of coal on our porch without saying a word. Daddy knew it was him, but Mr. Charles never took credit. That's just the kind of man he is." She smiled faintly, but there was something heavier behind it. "I don't think I ever thanked him properly. But maybe that's alright. Maybe the best way to thank someone like Mr. Charles is to keep showing up—just like he always did for us.

Eddie hadn't known Mr. Charles had a wife. He sat with the thought, picturing a younger version of the man he knew, standing in the same kitchen, cooking for someone else. 'What happened to her?' he asked.

Mama sighed, glancing at him briefly. 'She passed before you were born. Mr. Charles never left that house, though. It's like he just... stayed, kept doing what he always did.'

Eddie looked out the window, watching the trees blur past. The house had always felt old to him, but now it felt different. It wasn't just a house—it was a place filled with memories, with love that hadn't gone away, even when the people had. She spent a little more time talking to Mr. Charles now, asking him questions about the past, laughing at his dry wit. Eddie noticed how her hand lingered on his shoulder when she passed by, a silent gesture of care.

Eddie didn't say it out loud, but he knew things wouldn't always stay the same. The house, the cornbread, the quiet afternoons—they were all part of something that felt both steady and fragile. And as he walked out of the house that day, holding the last bite of corn-bread in his hand, he looked back at Mr. Charles sitting at the table, the sunlight catching the lines on his face, and he felt a strange mix of gratitude and sadness. He didn't have the words for it yet, but he knew he would never forget these moments. Did Mr. Charles feel it, too? Did he see the same quiet weight in Eddie that Eddie saw in him?

A RECIPE FOR REMEMBERING

MARION WADE

It was a rainy afternoon, the kind of day when the world outside felt muffled, wrapped in a blanket of mist. Eddie sat at Mr. Charles' kitchen table, watching raindrops streak down the window. Mama was in the next room, sorting through some papers Mr. Charles had asked her to look over.

"Mr. Charles?" Eddie asked hesitantly, breaking the quiet. "Can I ask you something?"

Mr. Charles, who had been carefully folding a dish towel, turned his head slightly. "You just did," he said, the corner of his mouth twitching into what Eddie had come to recognize as his version of a smile.

Eddie chuckled nervously. "No, I mean, something else. About your wife."

Mr. Charles' smile faded, replaced by a thoughtful expression. He pulled out the chair across from Eddie and sat down slowly, his hands resting on the worn tabletop. "What about her?"

Eddie hesitated, then plunged ahead. "What was she like? I mean, how did you two meet?"

Mr. Charles leaned back in his chair, staring at a spot somewhere past Eddie's shoulder. "We met at a church picnic," he said after a moment. "She was wearing a yellow dress, the color of sunshine. I thought she was the prettiest thing I'd ever seen. She had this way of laughing—not too loud, but just enough that you couldn't help but laugh with her."

Eddie rested his chin in his hand, waiting for more.

"We got married not long after. She used to bake pies—pecan pies that would make you forget your own name." Mr. Charles smiled faintly, his eyes still far away. "But she never got the cornbread right."

Eddie blinked. "She didn't?"

"Nope. She tried, bless her heart, but it just wasn't the same. I never did write it down, you see. It was something I learned from my grandmother, and I always did it by feel. She asked me a hundred times to teach her, but I told her it was the kind of thing you just had to know. She'd roll her eyes and call me a stubborn old fool."

Eddie couldn't help but laugh. "Did you ever tell her?"

Mr. Charles' expression softened. "Once, near the end, I tried. But she said she didn't want it written down—said if I ever taught someone, it should be by showing them. That's just how she was. Thought some things were better passed down that way. Eddie thought about that—how some things weren't meant to be written down, only shared. He wondered if that's why Mr. Charles had never tried to teach him, not yet. Maybe some things needed time before they were ready to be passed on."

Mr. Charles' hands stilled, his gaze shifting toward the far corner of the room. For a moment, he sat there, his expression unreadable, his lips parting slightly as if he meant to say something but thought better of it. Eddie followed his eyes but saw nothing—just an old wooden chair pushed neatly against the wall.

'Sometimes,' Mr. Charles murmured, barely louder than the rain tapping against the window, 'I still see her sitting there.'

Eddie's breath caught. He didn't know what to say, didn't know if he should say anything at all. The room felt heavier now, not in a sad way, but like it held something sacred. Like it was full of things that hadn't been spoken aloud in a long time.

Eddie was quiet for a while, watching as Mr. Charles picked up the towel and started folding it again. The rain pattered against the window, steady and calming.

"Thanks for telling me," Eddie said finally. "She sounds like she was pretty special."

Mr. Charles nodded slowly, his eyes meeting Eddie's. "She was," he said, his voice just above a whisper. "She sure was."

Eddie didn't say anything, but he felt it—that quiet kind of love that didn't fade, even after years had passed. And maybe, just maybe, Mr. Charles wanted him to know that.

MORE THAN CORNBREAD

MR. CHARLES' CORNBREAD

When Mama knocked on the door, it opened more slowly, and the warm smell of cornbread wasn't there to greet them. Eddie peered inside, his stomach twisting. The house felt quieter than usual, and Mr. Charles didn't look up as they entered.

"Charles?" Mama said softly, stepping into the kitchen. Mr. Charles was at the table, a thin blanket draped over his shoulders. He looked older, smaller somehow, as if the weight of his years had finally caught up to him.

"Hey, Charles," Mama said again, her voice gentle. She reached out to touch his shoulder, and he stirred, lifting his head to glance at her. His eyes were tired but still held that familiar spark. "We brought you some groceries."

Eddie stayed near the door, unsure of what to do. Mr. Charles' presence, once so steady and strong, seemed fragile now. Eddie watched as Mama moved around the kitchen, putting things away while speaking softly to Mr. Charles. He didn't say much, just nodded now and then, his voice barely a whisper.

After a while, Mama turned to Eddie. "Why don't you sit with Mr. Charles for a bit?" she said.

Eddie hesitated but then nodded. He pulled a chair out and sat across from Mr. Charles, who was looking down at his hands. They sat in silence for a long moment before Mr. Charles finally spoke.

"Thanks for coming by," Mr. Charles said, his voice rasping.

Eddie looked up. "Of course, Mr. Charles."

Mr. Charles gave him a small nod, his eyes scanning Eddie's face as if he wanted to say more. "You're a good boy," he said finally. "Your mama raised you right."

Eddie's cheeks warmed, and he ducked his head slightly. "Thanks, Mr. Charles."

"Eddie wanted to say more—to ask if Mr. Charles was feeling alright, to tell him he'd see him next time—but the words wouldn't come. Instead, he just sat there, memorizing the way Mr. Charles' fingers tapped lightly against the table, how his tired eyes held something unreadable.

"The kitchen felt smaller now, quieter, like it was holding its breath. The scent of cornbread wasn't in the air today, but Eddie swore he could still feel it there, lingering in the walls, in the creases of Mr. Charles' hands, in the quiet between their words.

Mama's voice gently broke the silence. 'Come on, baby, we should go.'

Eddie stood slowly. The chair scraped against the floor, the sound sharp in the hush of the kitchen. Mr. Charles didn't get up, but his eyes followed Eddie to the door. There was no big farewell, no extra words—just a small, slow nod."

When they left, Eddie felt a strange heaviness in the air, but he didn't think much of it at the time. The drive home was quiet, and Mama glanced at him occasionally through the rearview mirror, her expression unreadable.

Back home, as Eddie put his things away, Mama came into his room, a folded piece of paper in her hand.

"Eddie," she said gently. "Mr. Charles gave me this before we left. I think he meant it for you."

Eddie took the paper, unfolding it to find the recipe labeled "Mr. Charles' cornbread", written in careful, uneven handwriting. His chest tightened as he looked at the familiar scrawl.

Mama put a hand on his shoulder. "He wanted you to have it," she said softly. "Mama let out a quiet breath before speaking. 'Eddie... I don't think we'll be visiting Mr. Charles anymore.' She didn't look at him right away, just ran a hand over the folded paper in his hands like she was smoothing out something heavier than just a recipe."

Eddie stared at the recipe, his eyes prickling. He didn't say anything, just nodded as he clutched the paper tightly, feeling its weight as if it carried something more than just instructions. It carried memories, lessons, and the quiet strength of the man who had shared it.

Mama sat beside him, wrapping her arms around his shoulders. Eddie pressed his face into her side, letting the tears come. Her hand smoothed his hair, slow and steady, and she didn't say anything at first—just held him. The quiet weight of her comfort made it easier for Eddie to breathe again, even as the ache lingered. He clung to her warmth, feeling a little less alone in the moment. The recipe crinkled slightly in his grasp, and Eddie squeezed his fingers around it. He wasn't sure when he'd make it—if he'd ever make it—but he knew one thing: it was his now. And somehow, that meant Mr. Charles would never really be gone."

SOME THINGS NEVER FADE

MR. CHARLES

Eddie leaned back in his armchair, the recipe card resting on the table beside him. His grandson, a bright-eyed boy of about eight, sat cross-legged on the rug, listening intently. The room was quiet, the light from the kitchen faint and warm. Eddie's gaze rested on the recipe card beside him as the faint memory of cornbread baking seemed to linger in the air, a comforting echo of the past.

"Is that how it really happened, Grandpa?" the boy asked, his voice filled with a mix of doubt and wonder.

Eddie chuckled, the lines around his eyes softening. "What do you think?"

The boy tilted his head, his small fingers drumming against his knee. "It sounds like a story," he said. "But it smells real."

Eddie picked up the recipe card, his hand lingering on its worn edges. The paper was creased and faded, the ink faint, but the memories it held were as vivid as ever. He ran his thumb along the corner of the card, his gaze distant.

"Mr. Charles taught me more than how to make cornbread," Eddie said after a pause. "He taught me to slow down, to take my time and do things right. And that's something I've tried to live by ever since."

The boy leaned closer; his eyes fixed on the card. "Can I help you make the cornbread grandpa?"

"Maybe tomorrow," Eddie said, a soft smile playing on his lips. "I'll show you the way Mr. Charles showed me."

The boy nodded; his excitement tempered by a quiet understanding. Eddie placed the card back on the table, its edges frayed but its meaning undiminished. His fingers lingered for a moment before he pulled his hand away. It was just an old piece of paper, but it carried years of moments, laughter, and lessons. He glanced at his grandson, seeing a familiar spark of curiosity in his eyes—one he had once carried himself, sitting in a quiet kitchen with the scent of warm bread filling the air. The boy glanced at it, then back at his grandfather, the soft light from the kitchen reflecting off the worn surface. For a moment, the room felt still, almost sacred, as if the air itself was holding onto the story, the memory, the promise of another golden slice of cornbread.

And for a moment, he could almost hear Mr. Charles' low, gruff voice, feel the warm sun streaming through the kitchen window, and smell that first perfect batch of cornbread again.

Some things, he realized, never truly left you. They just became a part of who you were.